Mrs. Plug the Plumber

By Allan Ahlberg
Illustrated by Joe Wright

GOLDEN PRESS • NEW YORK
Western Publishing Company, Inc.
Racine, Wisconsin

First published in the United Kingdom by Puffin Books/Kestrel Books.
Published in the U.S.A. in 1982.

Library of Congress Catalog Card Number: 81-84171
ISBN 0-307-31706-4 / ISBN 0-307-61706-8 (lib. bdg.)
A B C D E F G H I J

Whenever a plumber
was needed in the town,
the people said,
"Send for Mrs. Plug!"

When Mrs. Plug was sent for,
Mrs. Plug came.

Mr. Plug came, too.

He was the plumber's partner.

Miss Plug and Master Plug
also came.

They were the plumber's babies.

Mrs. Plug had a useful bag.

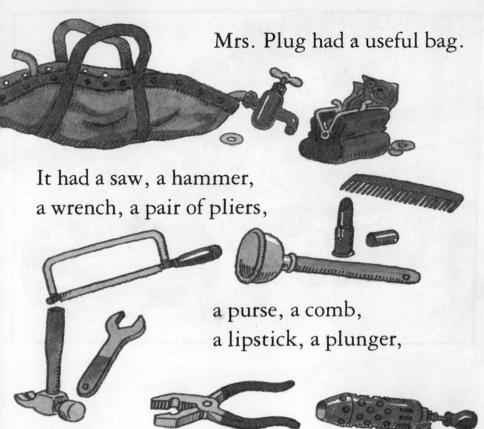

It had a saw, a hammer,
a wrench, a pair of pliers,

a purse, a comb,
a lipstick, a plunger,

a blowtorch
and a few other things in it.

One night there was some trouble
in a woman's bathroom.
A plumber was needed.
The neighbors said,
"Send for Mrs. Plug!"

Send for Mrs. Plug!

When Mrs. Plug was sent for,
Mrs. Plug came.
But this time Mr. Plug did not come.
He had to put the little Plugs to bed.

Mrs. Plug got on with the job.
When she finished it,
the woman gave her some money.
Mrs. Plug left for home.

On the way,
a terrible thing happened.
Mrs. Plug saw a robber.

He was robbing a rich man
in the street.
The robber saw Mrs. Plug.
He wanted to rob her, too.

"What's in that bag?" he asked.
"There's a comb," said Mrs. Plug.
"I will take that!" said the robber.
"And a lipstick," said Mrs. Plug.
"I will take that, too!" said the robber.
"And . . . a . . . blowtorch!"
said Mrs. Plug.

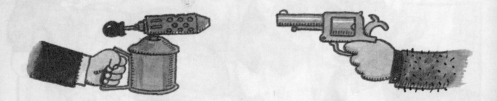

Then Mrs. Plug chased the robber
with her blowtorch.
She burned his bottom.
"Ouch!" the robber shouted.
And he ran off.

"That's a useful bag,"
the rich man said.
Then he said thank you to Mrs. Plug
and gave her a reward.
It was four tickets for a voyage
around the world.
   "I am in the steamship business,"
he said.

Mrs. Plug went home.
She told Mr. Plug about the robber
and the rich man.
She showed him the reward.
"You did very well, my dear,"
said Mr. Plug.
He gave her a cup of tea
and a kiss.

The next day Mrs. and Mr. Plug
got ready for the world voyage.
They packed their suitcases.
They asked a neighbor
to take care of the cat.
They put a note out
for the milkman.

Then off they went.
Mr. Plug carried the suitcases
and the little Plugs.
Mrs. Plug carried the useful bag.

The voyage began.
The Plug family had a good time.
They saw icebergs in the
northern seas.
They saw flying fish in the
southern seas.
They had dinner at the
captain's table.
They danced on deck
under the stars.

Then, one night,
a terrible thing happened.
There was a storm.

The ship hit a rock.
The rock made a hole
in the ship's side
and water poured in.

"Help, help!" the people shouted.
"We will all drown!"
They ran around
in their nightgowns and pajamas.
The captain looked at the hole.
"I think we need a plumber," he said.
"Send for Mrs. Plug!"
When Mrs. Plug was sent for,
Mrs. Plug came.
So did Mr. Plug and the little Plugs.
So did the useful bag.

Mrs. Plug got on with the job.
She used the wrench
and the hammer.
She used the pliers
and the blowtorch.
Mr. Plug helped her.
They both got soaking wet,
but they mended the hole!

All the people gathered around.

"Three cheers for the plumber
and the plumber's partner!"
the captain said.
"Three cheers for the plumber's babies!
Three cheers for the plumber's bag!"

The next night there was
a big celebration.
The Plug family had dinner
at the captain's table.
Mrs. and Mr. Plug danced on deck
under the stars.

The little Plugs stayed
with the captain.
They sat on his knee.
They played with his gold buttons
and his beard.

Suddenly the captain
felt his knee getting wet.
He looked at the little Plugs.
"I think one of you needs
a plumber," he said.
"Send for Mrs. Plug!"

The End